GOLDIBOOKS AND THE WEE BEAR

by TROY WILSON

Illustrated by
EDWARDIAN TAYLOR

RP|KIDS
PHILADELPHIA

To Lynn Wytenbroek,
whose children's literature classes at
Malaspina College in Nanaimo, BC,
were as good as gold and as great as honey.

Running Press Kids
Hachette Book Group
1290 Avenue of the Americas, New York, NY 10104
www.runningpress.com/rpkids
@RP_Kids

Printed in China

First Edition: January 2021

Published by Running Press Kids, an imprint of Perseus Books, LLC,
a subsidiary of Hachette Book Group, Inc. The Running Press Kids name and
logo is a trademark of the Hachette Book Group.

Print book cover and interior design by Frances J. Soo Ping Chow.

Library of Congress Control Number:2019948557

ISBNs: 978-0-7624-9620-4 (hardcover), 978-0-7624-9619-8 (ebook),
978-0-7624-7006-8 (ebook), 978-0-7624-7007-5 (ebook)

APS

10 9 8 7 6 5 4 3 2 1

Once there was a girl who thought books were
as good as gold. Everyone called her Goldibooks.

Her parents loved books, too.
They each had their own special bookshelves . . .

and their own special reading chairs.

One morning, they headed to the library to exchange some books.
Along the way, they spotted a wee bear.

“Awwwwww, it’s so cute!” said Goldi.

“Sure is,” replied Mom. “But remember, stay far away from wee bears.”

“Grown-up bears are dangerous if you get near their cubs!” explained Dad.

So they stayed far away.

Wee Bear, however, didn't even notice them pass by. He was desperately searching for something—*anything*—to read. Even a tiny scrap of paper would have been as great as honey.

After a while, he came upon a house. He knew he should quickly search the yard and leave, but he couldn't resist peeking inside.

And that's when he spotted . . . the bookshelves.
There must have been hundreds of books in there.

"Wow!" he gasped.

First, he tried Mom's books.

"Too hard!"

Then Dad's. "Too soft!"

Then Goldi's. "Just right!"

Now to find
a comfy spot to read.

First, he tried Mom's chair.
"Too hard!"

Then Dad's.
"Too soft!"

Then Goldi’s. “Just right!”

Or not . . .

Who knew finding a comfy spot to read could be so exhausting?
He decided to try reading in bed.

First, he tried Mom's bed.
"Too hard!"

Then Dad's. "Too soft!"

Then Goldi's. "Just right!"

After a few minutes, he fell fast asleep.

When Goldi and her parents returned home,
they were shocked!

“Someone’s been in my books,” said Mom.

“Mine, too,” said Dad.

“Mine, too,” said Goldi. “And they’re all gone!”

Then she spotted a trail.

“Someone’s been in my chair,” said Mom.

“Mine, too,” said Dad.

"Mine, too," said Goldi. "And it's broken!"

Then she spotted another trail.

“Someone’s been in my bed,” said Mom.

“Mine, too,” said Dad.

"Mine, too," said Goldi. "And they're still in it!"

Wee Bear woke with a start.

“What are you doing here?” asked Goldi.

“I know I shouldn’t have come in,” said Wee Bear, “but my family doesn’t have any b—”

"GRRRRRRRR!"

Everyone turned.

"How many times have we told you?"
growled Mama Bear. "Stay far away from wee humans."

“Grown-up humans are dangerous if you get near their kids,” growled Papa Bear.

“But look at all the books they have,” wailed Wee Bear.
“And we have none. It’s not fair!”

And that’s when Mama and Papa Bear
spotted the bookshelves.

"Wow!" Mama gasped.

"Double wow!" Papa gushed.

“Hey!” said Goldi. “Why don’t you all stay and read with us?”

“Can we?” asked Wee Bear.

“Um . . .” said Mama.

“Uh . . .” said Papa.

"Can they?" asked Goldi.

"Um . . ." said Mom.

"Uh . . ." said Dad.

"Pleeease?"
begged Goldi and Wee Bear.

"Well . . ." said Mom and Dad,
and Mama and Papa, ". . . Okay."

So they all read together.

And they did it the next week, too.

And the next.

And the next.

A few neighbors didn't know what to make of this new book club.

But most . . .

. . . thought it was just right!
THE END